copyright c 2008
by: Teresa M.F. Goodman

All rights reserved. No part of this publication may be copied, replaced, reproduced or transmitted in any form or by any means without permission of the author.

ISBN: 978-0-615-22092-5

Alchemy Studio
Art & Design
Creative Thought
Image & Words
Since 1970

## ACKNOWLEDGMENTS

Allow me to take this opportunity to first thank my father, John, for this rich and interesting heritage. It was his curiosity which inspired me to research and then write this book.

Secondly, to my husband, Jason, who drove the thousands of "klicks" around Ireland, patiently waited outside numerous libraries, pushed open rusty cemetery gates, climbed fences and took photos of it all. I especially want to thank him for his encouragement.

Finally to my Grandmother, Mary Magdalen and Katherine, my Great Grandmother, who really lived this story.

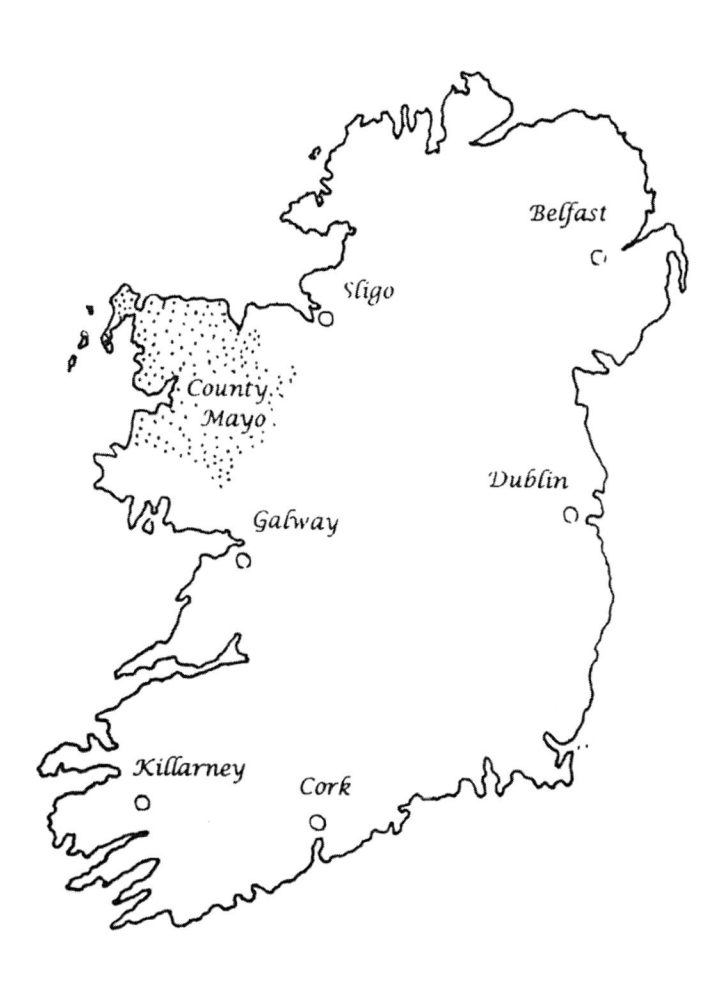

# IRELANDS MAGDALEN

## MARY MAGDALEN PADDON FEENY

The old homestead was full of dark dress and darker moods. Eleven children, now adults, had lost their Mother, Ma, as she was known by all. The home was still warm and comforting, but I could not smell that wonderful fresh baked bread she had made every day. I was young, only five, my cousins were numerous and ranged from teens to a newborn. My Aunts and Uncles were numerous as well. Six brothers there were, and five sisters. A great family of American born children to an Irish born Mother and a Father whose family left Ireland for England during the great famine of 1847.

Pa was still with us and a broken hearted man he was today. He had married the belle of Port Griffitth, and had a fruitful fifty years. Ma was gone, and that big house, so full of life, felt empty now.

We were all called out to the garden in the rear of the house, large enough to fit the extended family, for a talk. Time to tell stories, and even the youngest of us were anxious to get a seat nearest the storyteller. It was a beautiful late spring day, with fragrant flowers around, and with the house atop the only hill in town; we had an extraordinary view, facing south and down the Susquehanna River.

Pa, who usually was the first to speak, was to sit quietly this day. One of the elder children was to tell the first tale.

The wake for my Grandmother had begun.

In September 1881, Mary Magdalen Paddon was born in Ireland. Her Mother, Kit, was a young woman, only 16. This was her first child. Ireland was a struggling country at the time. Millions of people had left during the famine in 1847 and millions had died. The country was left with the hearty and the poor. It would only be a few years until Mary and her Mother would be leaving for North America themselves. Mary's father, John, would have a tragic death, and leave them on their own. It must have been a difficult choice, but Mary and her Mother were to set off for a new life in North America.

As a young woman, Mary emerges in a small yet prosperous town in a fertile valley in the American state of Pennsylvania. Her Mother has remarried and she now has a sister and a brother to live with. A few years of schooling were all she was to be given before she was old enough to find a way to make money to help her family. She became a domestic, and worked in one of the finest homes in Port Griffith. Once her talent for baking was discovered by her employers, she seldom again was asked to work in the laundry, or in the daily cleaning of the great house. But, with only the daily baking to do, she was left with more hours to fill with another position. Only a few blocks from her Mother and new Father's house was another fine home, away from the town center, and at the top of the hill on Chapel Street. The Feeny home was a large full house! With a successful Irish family, supported by sons and daughters who came to America, one by one, as the family could afford, finally able to bring their aging parents from England. The Mother was ailing and so a domestic was brought in to help prepare meals. Mary was hired and she was about to meet some very important men in her life.

Thomas and Michael were the two providers in the Feeny family; two brothers, who had brought their family to America. Their father had been a successful cabinetmaker back in England and was able to find work in the growing town of Port Griffith. Their mother, speaking only Irish, kept the household in order, with some outside help. Margaret Feeny had not been well even before leaving England for America and was growing weaker. Perhaps her ill health was the reason she was to say she never really liked America, perhaps because it separated her family, as she still had her oldest son and his family in Leeds, England.

Son Michael had the slight build of his Mothers side of the family, but he made up for his stature by dressing in a suit every day. He was the talker and storyteller, and found himself a position at the local newspaper, the Port Griffith Dispatch.

Son Thomas inherited the larger, stronger frame of his Fathers side of the family. Capable and willing to do the more physically demanding tasks. After a brief time of working in the Anthracite coal mines in the area, he found himself in a position of great respect and substantial income as an engineer on the Pennsylvania Railroad and worked on the Black Diamond Train. There was a growing rivalry between the brothers, when beautiful Mary came to assist their mother in running the house, although great brotherly love allowed both to stand back and let Mary make her choice.

Kit Paddon herself had married again in America. She met a dashing solder from World War I, who came home a hero, but was plagued by the events he witnessed. He often was to turn to alcohol in an attempt to erase his memories. There were to be a brother and a sister brought into Mary's, until now somewhat quiet world. She was to cherish her siblings and was a willing worker to help in the financial upbringing of the two. But the disruption of the family was to be her new father, Peter McAndrew.

A night of drinking brought out his very violent side of which he brought home to his family. It was to be Kit who suffered the most, with drunken rages he would leave her bruised. Kit was scared, and was never to tell a sole what went on in their small house at the base of the hill. It was an event that was accepted in those days, a woman never ever gave it a thought to leave her home, especially when she had no other family members of her own to go to for shelter.

Mary was in audience to these episodes often, and carried the fear and shame with her. Perhaps this was one reason why the strong, protective Thomas Feeny would steal her heart and make her his bride. Kit and the children were to be liberated as well, as one drunken night Peter McAndrew, the War Hero, was to meet his death at the bottom of the cellar stairs. No doubt on his way down for another bottle of his favorite whiskey.

The Feeny family opened their arms to their new member. By now all of Thomas' sisters were married and with children of their own. Once heartbroken, Michael too had found a new love in his life and he was to be married. All the Feenys had stayed in the general area of Port Griffith, creating a strong family bond.
Mary was not to know her future Mother-in-law for very long, as Margaret Feeny passed away shortly after Mary was employed in the home. It would take more than one woman to run such a house, so Thomas sister Annie moved back home. Mary and Annie became fast friends.
The Feeny family had joined the Catholic Church, Saint Mary's, down near the river. The cemetery was above the town center, a few miles away. It would only be two more years before their Father Michael himself was to be placed next to his wife, as he too passed away.
Both these parents had witnessed the famine in Ireland, had struggled through the near starvation of their brothers and sisters. Their parents, the Feenys and the Corcorans, had been neighbors in Ireland. The fathers had been craftsmen together. As close friends and business partners they left the West of Ireland in1845 for England. With two large families, it was an easier trip by the measure of time and money to go across the Irish Sea and settle in Leeds, England. Only when the sons reached the age to work did the dream of going to America become a reality.

The first exodus of the Feeny children was to be the oldest girl, Annie, her husband George Bentley, and the two brothers; Michael and Thomas. Living with the Bentley family until work was found, the boys soon found a house of their own and sent for their parents. The other sisters were to follow over the next few years. It was only Phillip, the oldest, who was never to come, and was thought to be lost for many years. Some thought he drank up the fare sent to him, others thought it was his own children who kept him in England and still others said he left everyone behind and continued to California.

There was more bad luck to fall on the extended family of Feenys. Their sister Hanna passed away leaving a set of twin girls and a son to care for. Annie was to take in the three of them, joining the three of her own. Love and determination were to be passed to another generation.

With Annie, her husband, their children and Hanna's children living in the homestead, it was time for Thomas to move into his own home. After Mary and Thomas wed, they found a small brick house near the railway station, only a few miles from the house on the hill. There, Mary was to have three of their eleven children.

Upon the death of their father Michael Feeny, son Thomas, Mary Magdalen and their children, Katherine, Mike and Mary were to move back into the homestead at the top of the hill. They were a happy and prosperous family. Thomas, or as he was now called, Pa, continued to establish himself with the Pennsylvania railroad and provided quite well for his growing family. And Ma continued to bake loaves of bread for a store in town, bringing in her own share of the income. Eight more children were to be a gift to the family. All were to go to school till their own employment meant more. The youngest of the family were to graduate from High school, a great accomplishment in those days. Many of the boys and the girl's husbands were to go to war, and with great fortune all returned.

Ma and Pa's home was to be the center of the family during World War II. Many of the married sisters and the brother's wives lived there with their children. Family members from as far away as Washington DC came back to wait for the war to end. Grandchildren were born there, and relatives were waked there. That is the way it was then. Family was everything, and everything was for the family. When the war ended all returned home, most settling nearby, but a few were drawn back to the big cities for a better job. The oldest boy, Mike, opened a local café, which was soon to be a second home to the men in the family. Perhaps it was the war that brought them together there; of course a good beer and a chat with your brother could make your day. Mike and his wife, Dora lived upstairs from the "beer garden". It was a great 1920's design apartment, very elegant, and home to their three children.

All the brothers would take turns tending the bar, and their children were to find themselves there for hours, playing shuffleboard and checkers, and if allowed, spending time in the forth floor attic of the great building.

Katherine, and her husband Mickey, a brilliant man who worked for the railroad industry, had moved away from Pennsylvania, where he found a position in Washington DC, there they raised their son Terence. Mary, who was a beauty like her Mother, married Bill and raised their son Billy, within only a few miles from the homestead. Mary, found a position with the telephone company, a great job in those days, and went on to train people for the position of telephone operator. Thomas 2$^{nd}$ and Anne Feeny had their own tragedy, as they lost their only son to an automobile accident. But daughter Anne was to provide them with fine grandchildren.

Joseph Feeny was very much like his Uncle Mike, slight in build, but full of poetry and the gift of gab, he and Alice had a lovely daughter Patsy. William, or as his family called him, Chief, was the only bachelor of the family, a tall man, with deep voice and demanding ways, his nieces and nephews loved him.

Francis Feeny was the most handsome of the boys. He had the dark hair and blue eyes of his Grandfather Michael. He was smart and social, and besides owning his own "Pub", he got involved with local politics and was voted into the office of city councilman. He married a lovely woman, smart as well, and had three great kids. John was the youngest of the boys. He met his West Virginia born wife in Washington DC, before the war while they both worked at Kresge's. Anna and her first daughter, Barbara, lived in the Feeny homestead while John was fighting in WW ll. Upon his return, they settled in Port Griffith and had three more girls; Maureen, Teresa and Kathleen.
Margarette had met her husband in the DC area and settled there, and raised two boys and a girl.
Anne had married the dashing Bob, a WW II pilot, who became an active member of the local community; they were to have three girls.
Alice married a Port Griffith man and also had two boys and a girl. It was Alice who would make the homestead her lifetime home. So there certainly was a large enough audience for every story, and for every performance put on by the children.

## TELLIN' of the TALES

Pa was the one to tell the tales of the Irish in Ireland. How his father, Michaels' childhood was so poor and nearly fatal. Michael's father Bartholomew was a weaver and was able to take care of his family until the English forced the Catholics to the most remote parts of Ireland in County Mayo. Without the ability to earn a living coupled with the blight of the potato crop for three years, there was nothing left to do but leave Ireland, so the entire family moved to England. A difficult decision to make, going to a country that was so prejudice against you, but it was the closest and the least expensive to travel to. Thomas, our Pa, and his eight brothers and sisters were born in England, yet were very proud to call themselves Irish! When the children became adults they too were ready to immigrate, not back to Ireland, but to America, so the exodus began.

Finding employment in the Susquehanna Valley, allowed the Feeny brothers to send for their parents. A few of their sisters had already made the journey with their husbands and they all were doing well. Buying the hilltop house was a great day for the boys, and they were proud to welcome their parents to the home. Just as thousands of others, their Irish family had successfully started a new life in America. The house was to be a shelter to many and a solid foundation for the Feeny family. Babies were born there, and people were to die there.

Pa's sister Catherine was to have the first wake in the Feeny household. Her husband was killed, hit by a train. It was a tragic time, and Catherine never forgave the country, which brought the death of her husband. The next year she was to return to England. It was to be years again till the family heard from her. And years before the family found out the story of their missing brother Phillip. On her return to England she had found her brother Phillip and family. So the mystery of Phillip was solved, Phillip's wife would not leave England, having three children of their own, she was too fearful of a trip across the ocean. Phillip showed his sister the ticket, old and tattered, that he purchased to bring his family to America, but his wife refused to leave. The Feenys in America thought their brother had drunk up the money or gambled it away, leaving them angry and him isolated.

Stories of the Feenys, they were many...but what of the story of the Paddons?  Yes, Ma, had come to America as a young girl, and really had few memories of Ireland, yet her mother, Kit should have had many a story.  But there were to be none. Her stories were vague and short.  She claimed to be from County Sligo.  What she did reveal was that her Mothers maiden name was Day, and fathers name Ward, and her husbands, who drown, was John Paddon.   No stories of a trip across the ocean, the stop over in Canada, or why they chose the Susquehanna Valley to settle.    And so only the Feeny side of the family was the history to be known.

Ma's mother Kit was also to move to the Feeny house in her last years.  Half a lifetime of Diabetes led to the amputation of her right leg.  She was to spend the last year in bed, waited on by Ma and helped by the women then living in the house.  Many a story was to go with Kit to the grave.  Many a secret was to be unknown to the family and as well as to Ma herself.  Yes, there was to be speculation as to the past of Kit.  As a young woman in her early twenties, she brought her five-year-old daughter across the Atlantic Ocean to begin a new life.  How and why?

What was the history of her life in Ireland?

.

## John in IRELAND

Of all the Feeny children, only one was to return to Ireland, long after Ma and Pa had passed away. Returning to the old sod in 1990 was the youngest son John, his wife, Anna, daughter Teresa and her husband Jason. Many of the facts of the Feeny family were known, and enabled John to find his Grandfathers home in County Mayo, in the Parish of Kilbride, "Bridgets Church". Walking through many a cemetery in the parish, John was able to find old tombstones with the Feeny name. Michael Feeny, whose father was Bartholomew, was born in 1836, ten years before the height of the dreadful famine. Bartholomew, or Bartley, was able to take his family to England, and therefore spare the lives of his family.

Kilbride was a beautiful coastal town, near Killala Bay and John Feeny was so proud to stand on the ground of his forefathers.

But, there still remained the mysteries of his Grandmother and his Mother's homeland. A professional search was done by an agency from Ireland, but nothing was found. No person of that name was found in county Sligo. So, John and Teresa set out to do their own research.

A trip to Dublin, and hours in the library was to follow. Could Kit have been wrong about Mary's place of birth? Perhaps a search of another county would help. So the Father and daughter team did a detailed search. But again, nothing was found in County Clare, Mayo, Kerry, Galway, all the western counties. There was to be no record of a birth of Mary Magdalen Paddon.

The next try would be to find the birth of Kit, surely those records could be found. Again, County Sligo was the first to be checked. That is where she said she was from. A common name, Ward, there was bound to be many. A professional search was again done, given the contradictory information the family had; this search was becoming very difficult and quite mysterious. Was her Mothers maiden name Day? Why could they not find her record of marriage to John Paddon?

Time was running out, for Johns visit to Ireland was coming to an end. Further research would have to be done from the United States. So close, yet still so far from the true story.

## The Research Begins

The year now is 2000. John has passed away, still not knowing the history of his dear Mother. Kit and Mary Magdalen had carried their histories to their graves. Had any of the older children of Ma's known the story? Was there something to hide? John's daughter, Teresa was to continue the search. Teresa and her husband Jason were to travel to Ireland and stay for four months. With the desire to finish her fathers search, she was determined to solve this mystery. Since Mary Magdalen was not to be found, the key to the search would be Kit, Kit Ward Paddon. A search found twenty Katherine Wards born in Ireland in the years from 1863 to 1865. On Kits death certificate was the year 1863, on her marriage certificate to Peter McAndrew, was the year 1865. It was decided to try the middle ground and begin the search in 1864. There was found a Katherine Ward born May 22, parents were Patrick and wife Ellen Loftus. Kit claimed her mother's maiden name was Day, but that was not really an Irish name. What had she so wanted to cover up?? The birth took place in a western town in County Mayo, Belmullet. Perhaps a trip to the area would give us some answers.

Traveling to Belmullet, takes you through some of the most bleak and barren land in western Ireland. Historical letters told of the land being striped of all trees by the Vikings for their ships. In 1800, it was said of the inhabitants, they had never seen a tree, a bridge, or a flight of stairs, although they could speak six languages, paint, sing and play piano! The mountains end and there seems to be endless areas of bog. An extremely isolated place it must have been, back before the automobile. The nearest town of Ballina was 35 miles away. Yes, and another 35 miles to the port city of Sligo, in county Sligo! A port used by many an Irishman to sail to America. Sligo, also the county Kit claimed to be from. Belmullet was a coastal town, but its shoreline was rough and too dangerous for a large harbor. One would have to make the seventy-mile journey to leave Ireland by ship. But Belmullet was quite beautiful. The Mullet, as it is called, is a strand of land three miles long and less than one mile wide at its widest point. Off the coast are two islands, North and South Inishkea, deserted now, but once the home to two prevalent families, Loftus on the north island and on the south, the Wards.

Kilmore parish was where the local history could be researched. After looking through pages and pages of old documents we found what we believed was what we had been looking for. There was a Katherine Ward baptized in May of 1864, who's Father was Patrick Ward and Mother Ellen Loftus, and the Godparents were James Murphy and Bridget Gerrity. Katherine was born on a small island off the coast of Bellmullet named Inishkea. Katherine had a brother Anthony, and two sisters, Honor and Rose. Unfortunately, no other records of the family were found. No marriage or death certificates, leading to the belief the family had emigrated. But hadn't Kit and her daughter traveled to America alone as was believed by the family and Mary herself? Where had the family gone, and why were they separated? What was the secret they carried?

## INISHKEA ISLAND

Inishkea Island was a beautiful and remote place. Barely a mile in length and 300 yards wide, it was the tip of the West coast of Ireland, the buffer at the edge of the Atlantic. There were two parts to the Island North and South. At rare times when the mighty ocean was calm, there was a narrow inlet exposed, connecting the two. At that time the clans from each would cross over and meet. They were friends and many of the families had married and essentially joined the islands. It is said that when the currents were high and strong, and the winds fearsome, lovers would sing to each other across the inlet. The highs and lows of the singing voice would be carried by the winds.

The family homes were on the east side, the more sheltered side of the island. There were beaches and even a harbor for ships that would come to buy lobster and fish from the islanders, or for those who came for safety, in times of storms. The islanders themselves only went to the mainland for goods not provided by the island, such as flour, sugar, tea and stout. But their life on the island provided them with much. They had sheep and cattle, chickens and geese; the sea gave them the rest. They ate lobster and clams, mussels and salmon. They had good soil on the island as well and grew cabbage, carrots, parsnips, onions and of course the potato. The hills were perfect for the "lazy beds" as they were called. To enrich the soil, they added manure, lime rich seashells and seaweed.

The Inishkea people were healthy, but not wealthy. They were able to live off the earth and sea and they could trade for items from the mainland, but money was something hard to come by. The most profitable of goods they made was a dye, a dark purple, made from shellfish, seaweeds, jelly-fish and starfish; a dye very much in demand at the time by royalty and nobility.  There were also times when the men of the island could earn high wages by working off the island.  It would take them away from home for three months at a time, and it left the women and young boys alone.  In the fall of the year, there was a great demand for workers in the fish canneries in Scotland. The men would be paid well and all were willing to go, the young men especially looked forward to the adventure.  A lot had to be done to be prepared for the absence of the men.  Storage supplies were put in, as all of the necessities had to last until mid-December, when the men would return. And when they did, they brought some special treats; besides money, the rare and loved coffee and chocolate!  It was an experience that the women also looked forward to. They met in each of their homes and told stories. They went from house to house, spinning wool for the looms, producing flannels and tweeds.  They sang and played instruments. But they kept their rifles near.  They were a quite fearless group of women, experiencing a lot in their isolated lives and were prepared for anything.

Years ago the only visitors were the shipwrecked sailors who swam to shore.  If the sailors made it through the ordeal, they were brought to the mainland. Meanwhile the islanders filled their homes and caves with the spoils of the wreck.  The women were just as willing to reap the benefits of a wrecked ship.  It provided furniture, glass, pots and dishes from some of the grandest Spanish Armadas!   Not only the Spanish, but the French and Scandinavian ships also found the Belmullet coast to be dangerous.  Many would be destroyed on its rocky coast.  But many of these seafarers found the country and the women quite beautiful and made Ireland their home.

The islanders could tell when a storm was approaching.  They were so gifted in reading the sky and the sea, their sight and hearing being quite acute.  Upon their warnings, the island families would go to their sheltered homes and wait for the storms to pass.  The homes all had a room nestled into the earth, with solid walls and stocked with supplies.  Many times the island had to be rebuilt after a severe ocean storm, some destroying homes and even killing people, but the islanders would not leave the place they loved so.

COUNTY MAYO, IRELAND c. 1875

## AUTUMN 1880
## THE MULLET

Katherine sat on the highest rock near the southern part of the island. It was cold and she had to wrap herself completely to keep out the winds. With her back to a large stone she was as protected as she could be. From this vantage point she could see the mouth of Blacksod Bay, and any vessel that should be on it. It was Sunday and he always could be seen coming around noon. She watched for him on many days, but this was the day he would stop on her island. She had been watching him for many months now. Always alone, he was a curiosity. It would take many weeks before she got a good look at him. From a distance, she could only see his silhouette, large shoulders and a long back, a powerful sight, rowing and conquering the waves. Other men and boys had come to the island, but none had caught her eye. Her Father had his eye on a young man for her, from the mainland, Liam Burke, who worked in his own father's mill. Liam was of marrying age, just as Kit was becoming. On her next birthday she would be 16, and time for her, by tradition, to start her own family. Marriages were arranged by the parents, and until an agreement was made the young man could not propose. Love matches were rare, money was the deciding factor. But her dreams were of the man approaching in his currach. Why would she want to leave the island and live in the town with the young Liam Burke? She would be away from the majestic sea and her island. Her eyes again caught sight of the mysterious man in his boat. He had been to the island many times to deal with the men. Had he noticed her at all? Each time he came on shore, she was drawn closer and closer. His age, she could not tell. He had the face of a weathered fisherman, skin roughed by the wind and sea. His hair was black and yes, he was tall and strong. She would watch while he brought ashore his boat, one strong pull was all it took. Today if he stopped it would be different, no man was on the island, as it was October and they were all off to foreign lands to earn money.

She ran to the harbor, as today she decided she would speak to him. He lifted his head to see her standing there, quite a sight to him. A young woman wrapped in many shawls of just as many colors, long blond hair blowing in all directions, like the rays from the sun! He laughed at the sight!

Their first meeting and he laughs?  She immediately became angry; this was not the romantic meeting she had dreamed of.  What do you want here? Do you not know men are not allowed on the island till Christmas?  You should be gone before a bullet is put into you!

I have only stopped to bring this box for the woman Ward.  Liam Burke, in town, gave it to me; he paid me to deliver it.
Which Ward is it then? There are many of us.
I was told to give it to the pretty one.  I was thinking that must be you.

Kit was afraid she blushed at those words coming from him.
I cannot take that from you or him, as my father is not here to accept it.
Perhaps we can hide this away somewhere until the men return, and your father can decide if you should accept this man and his gift.
And from who am I to say delivered this box?
My name is John Paddon.
She sat on the edge of the wall and sat silently, looking him over as he tied his boat and seemed to be making himself comfortable.
Are ye planning to stay then?
Well, I cannot leave until I finish the job I've accepted payment to do.  I shall deliver this to the female head of the Ward clan. Can you tell me which house it is?

Sure, though there is no one there today, all the woman are in the north island finishing the weaving  Perhaps I can help you to hide the box, until the men return.
And am I to trust a woman as you, who cannot even give me her name?  And trust that you yourself would not keep the box?
You must trust me and I shall tell you my name, I am the daughter of Patrick Ward, my name is Kit.
He stared at her a long time, as if trying to judge her age, her figure under the shawls, her spirit and, if any, her fear.  The only thing clear to him was her blue, inquiring eyes.

Do you like living out here then, away from all the activity of the town; the dances, the parties, the boys?
We have most all of that here, I miss nothing.
Well, you do have a great island here.  Your family keeps to themselves, keeps others out, and keeps some of their treasures hidden, like yourself.

Give me the box then.
No, I believe the proper thing to do is give this to your father. I'd like to keep it here on the island till he returns, as I would not like it to end up on the bottom of the ocean, perhaps being tossed from my boat. I should like to bury it at the Holy Well, and would like you to wait here while I do so. Too tempting it would be for you to know of its location!

Go ahead then, as am I not too eager to want to see what is in the box anyway. I can wait here.

He took off towards the cave and soon was out of sight. The Holy Well was a sacred place, with a fresh water spring, Holy to the ancient Celts, and the only thing nearest a church on the island.
She was very much attracted to this John Paddon, he was much older that her fifteen years, but she believed she was very grown up, and did not care. She wondered if her Mother would allow him to come into the house as she did not want to see him leave too soon. He was approaching the boat launch again, walking slowly, tall and strong in silhouette. She wondered how he would kiss. She had never been really kissed, not by a man, only by boys in games. She was eager to have someone hold her and kiss her, and it was difficult to hide her desires.
Are you sure you did not follow me and see where I hid the gift? Or, maybe you really are not interested in the young Mr. Burke.

I don't think I need tell you my interest sir.

That does not surprise me, lady, as I think you have a good deal hidden from me already.

He stared out towards the sea, and began to ready his boat for departure.

Will you come for a ride on the sea then miss?
She had to stop herself from jumping up and into the boat. Although she could not really see why she should not, as she very much wanted to, and she was not finished with this man yet.

And if were to go with you, how am I to be sure you would not take me to Inishglora and hide me in a well or Poteen cave?

(Inishglora was a small island even further out into the Atlantic, with a rocky surface and plenty of caves to hide the homemade whiskey.)

Ha! No it would be better if I were to take you to my cottage to cook and work for me.
That will not do, not for a man as grown as you, and who seems to not need anyone to help him. You do not have a wife then?
No, I am a bachelor, with no woman in my house. I have not taken a wife as I spend too much time on the sea, and I have no time to be in town pubs or church socials to meet one. Well, I am off now dear miss Kit Ward, perhaps we shall meet again when the men return.
He was in the boat now and heading off. Kit walked down to the waters edge, threw off the shawl from her head and let her long blond tresses cover her shoulders.

You needn't wait that long, you may need to come and be sure I have not found the box. Perhaps you may need to return it to Mr. Burke.
She could read his expression; he was pleased and interested.

Well then, I shall see you again soon. Be good!


All of the girls and women were home that evening. Kit was reprimanded for not being with the others to help with the weaving. She used the sheep as an excuse to her Mother. She said three of them had been isolated on the rocks when the tide came in and she had to lead them one by one through the water back to shore. Her Mother paid little attention to the excuse as Kit was often going off on her own, not liking to sit with the other women of the island. Her Kit was an independent one, not like her daughter Honor, who was married and pregnant with her first child. Honor liked to be inside and had set up a lovely cottage for herself and her husband. She could cook and kept a clean home.

Kit was happier out of doors, and was up and out as soon as possible each day. She preferred to work with her Father in the fields or with the stock. She never showed much interest in the homebound duties of a wife. But hers was an accepted behavior, as the first boy in the family was still very young. Kit was a great help to her Father. She helped with the outdoor duties and was the only girl on the island to have her own pony.

Kit lay in bed that evening, going over and over the entire meeting with this John Paddon. It pleased her that she felt he was interested in her. But she regretted, in retrospect, not throwing the box into the sea. Or telling him she had no interest at all in the boy Liam Burke. She was sorry she hadn't followed him to the hiding place. Tomorrow she would go and look for it. John Paddon...where did he live? Could she make it to his cottage on the mainland if she tried? Should she try to handle a currach by herself, they were a light weight canvas boat, usually requiring two men to handle one in rough waters. She had better not try. Tonight she wished she could fly!

The few days that followed felt like an eternity to Kit. Every high tide she found a place near the shore to look for him in the distance. Three long days had passed and no sight of him. Sometimes she felt it a curse living on this island. If on the mainland a long walk could be taken, or an inquiry could be made as to where he lives. A trip to the mainland could be made, but it was not very safe for a woman to try it alone. A few women in the boat could insure the strength to return, as the sea was not to be trusted to remain calm. A storm could come up very suddenly and turn boat over. No, there was only the option, to wait, so wait she did.

On the high tide of the fourth day, she saw a boat in the distance. It looked like one man; perhaps it was John. It could be an hour before he would be near enough to see clearly.

Her heart leaped! He was headed toward the harbor, and she would greet him!
He seemed to expect her presence, not at all surprised, but she didn't care, she was not going to hide her interest. And neither did he!

Beautiful day, how are you getting on, pretty girl? Have you dug holes all over the island trying to find the mysterious box?

I have told you, I do not care about it. The pigs could dig it up and eat it and not bother me. Have you come to dig it up yourself then?
No, I'm just stopping on my way to the North Island, where I am to deliver this turf. Is there anything you or your family need from the mainland? There is talk of bad weather in the next few days, so if you let me know now, I'll be sure to get back tomorrow.

Well, we had better ask the women of the island, the heads of the house while the men are away.
Together they walked toward the Grandmother Ward's home. When the house was in view, Kit took a seat on a stone wall and told him he must go on alone.  She wanted to see if this man would be asked into the house, and he was.  So, the clan trusts him, she decided.  Good, as she wanted him to be accepted.  He was not gone too long, and returned to the place where she sat.

Thank you for waiting for me, did you fear I would not come out alive!  You see, I have known Mrs. Ward for many years, and do what I can for her.
As they neared the boat ramp, he took her hand.  She flushed with excitement!  It was the first time for her to feel this way.  At first she felt a bit of fear, but with growing interest, she held on tight.

Must you go so soon?  You have a few hours of daylight in which to make your journey and return to the mainland.

I live within Tullagh Bay, and must get back before the low tide; otherwise I will be walking in the depths of mud!  But if you do like my company, I shall be returning tomorrow, and can come early and sit with you.

I would like that, and I will bring a basket, with fruit and bread for us to share.  And we can dig up the box and throw it into the sea!

He lifted her chin and got so close; she wanted to close her eyes in preparation of a kiss.  But he just tapped her on the nose and he was off.


Did her Mother notice how early she was up and how quickly her chores were done?  She awoke with such eagerness these days. And she really wondered if this is what was called love.  She was obsessed with the thought and desire of him.  She had never felt this way before.  Her mind and her body were ready for a man. Not a boy as was Liam Burke, the gift giver.  She wanted a man, strong and protective, one with excitement, and passion, she was ready for passion!

He was there the next day, with the goods that Grandmother Ward had requested. Kit did not meet him, as she so much wanted to. Instead she waited, out of sight, wanting to see if he looked for her. He went about tying his boat and unloading the goods for Mrs. Ward. He seemed to stop and move along quite slowly, perhaps waiting for Kit to show herself.

Kit let him deliver the goods, and waited for his return from the house.

She fussed with her hair and tightened her bodice. She pinched her cheeks and pressed her lips to make them blush. He came towards the harbor, he had a shaved face and it made her smile and feel confident. She rose to her feet when he was near. His pace quickened. She so very much wanted to run to him and be taken up in his arms, but she waited. His approach slowed, and he seemed unsure. This made her call out to him, trying to mask her eagerness with humor.

Has the woman thrown you out? Is she loading the rifle to come after you? Must I hide you in the well or the still? Take my hand, and he did.


They walked towards the very southern tip of the island. There were some flat rocks perfect for sitting and watching the Atlantic Ocean. He helped her down to a seat just above the crashing of the waves. It was a beautiful sunny day, yet chilly in the November wind. He sat next to her and put his arm around her shoulder. She wanted to melt in his arms; this must be what is known as love. He told her about himself as they sat there. He was a loner, with no family; all had immigrated to Australia. Yet, he had stayed; content to live off the sea and his small bit of land. He had a cottage deep in Tullagh Bay, within the bog. The tide dictated when he could take to the sea, as he had to do so in high tide. But the bog also protected him from all sides, so his home was a safe haven to him.

She felt his warmth and could breathe in his scent, which was smoky and salty.  She could barely speak and was ready to let go of any defenses she should have in the presence of this man.  He brought her face around to his and kissed her, first lightly; perhaps waiting to see her reaction, then deeply, as she eagerly participated.  She could taste him now, and feel his body so close.

You are a very desirable girl, Kit Ward....I don't know if this is right for us to be here as we are, but I do want to be next to you.  I don't even want to ask your age, as I do not want anything to come between us seeing each other.  It probably is not what your family would want you to be doing, kissing an older man as myself.

I do not care what my family thinks or wants for me, I can decide for myself. I do not want to stop seeing you, while my father is away.  He will be gone for two more months, too long to not be kissed again.

They sat together silently; he staring out to sea, she staring at his hands, his clothes, his hair and profile; she loved him.

The next few days were dark and windy; the storm had lingered on the west coast.  Even the sheep and cattle had to be kept enclosed, and Kit had to be patient until she could see John again.  She kept it a secret from her Mother and even her oldest sister, Honor, with whom she was quite close.  She knew with her Father away, she should not be seeing a man alone.  But she could take care of herself, she always had.  She was more independent that any of the girls in the family, and was proud of that.

Many days had passed before she again saw a currach approach the island.  It was John and she could not stop herself from running to him.  He jumped from his boat, gave it one huge tug and it was on shore.  He turned just in time to catch her in his arms.  They kissed, long and passionately. I've stopped to take you with me on an adventure, can you get away?

Of course, I am more than ready for an adventure! They headed for the island of Inishglora.  No one lived on it, and it was only used as a stop for fisherman who needed shelter from a storm. There were numerous "Bee-hive" cells used by the Monks of St. Brendan's church many years ago, some which you could still enter.

It was about an hour's journey if the seas were with you.  It was an exhilarating ride!  They reached the shore when the sun was high overhead.  John picked up a cloth sack and a bottle and they set off for a fine green spot.  He seemed to know his way around the place, and he soon found a sheltered area with a tree, bent towards the shore, the way the wind had forced it to grow.  A "cell" and a fresh water spring were nearby.  He opened the sack and brought out some bread, cheese and, a great treat, oranges!  The bottle was one of home brew poteen.  They sat and told stories and laughed, she was enchanted.   For days she had been preparing for a meeting as this.  Her hair was glistening clean, her clothes smelled of heather, and her skin was pink and glowing.

She was bursting inside with wanting to give herself to him.

When their lunch had finished and a few sips of the bottle had been taken, they fell into silence, this was to be the time, he knew she was ready and he had been waiting so long for them to be alone like this.  No threat of a sister or little brother coming around the corner, no other fisherman, just the two of them.

He pulled her close, and she slipped her hand on to his bare chest.

## CHRISTMAS 1880

Father would be returning soon, as would the rest of the men from the island. Honor was so excited, as her husband would soon be home. Kit was there to help her get the house ready for his arrival, and in decorating for the Christmas season. Pies and even candy were made, and all available bottles were filled with the islands best poteen. Honor was soon to give birth and Kit had been living with her sister for the past few weeks. She had once put aside all of her sisters doings as girlish and frivolous. But these days she had her own dreams of having a home and a husband, she no longer dallied in the fields with the stock, or languished on the west coast watching the open sea. She only thought of how and when she would see him again. She was no longer a girl, she was a woman, had become so that day on Inishglora. Her concern now was with when she could go to John's home and stay with him. He had not yet talked of marriage, but maybe that was because her father was away. Kit would have to wait for the time she could speak with her father and tell him of her love for this man John Paddon.

She had told her sister of John, a man that she would like Honor to meet. She told her stories of how he would visit the island, and of course just sit in his boat and talk, as she knew he could not come on shore until the men returned!

Honor knew their father had already arranged Kit's marriage to Liam Burke, and tried to stop her sister's attention to this unknown man. But it was too late, she could see in Kit's eyes, she was in love.

The men returned, Christmas was celebrated and weeks went by without a sight of John Paddon. Kit was devastated. Where was he? She finally told her father of a fisherman she met, whom she would like to have her father's permission for him to call on her. Her father knew more of John Paddon than Kit realized. He began to tell her of him.

He was 45 years old, and a sick man! Still a bachelor, because a woman could not trust him, with this strange illness; he had fit's, and was a danger to be with. She remembered once seeing him lying in is boat, shaking and quivering, she did not know what happened and he dismissed the event by saying he had a fever. Oh, but where was he now, she needed to see him and be with him. Her Father was on his way to the mainland. She so wanted to go, but he refused to let her. He would find John Paddon and speak to him, and was also going to see Liam. She sat outside of her sister's cottage, waiting for their fathers return. Kit could not help but to feel envy of her big sister. Now she wanted a husband, a child, a house, the kind of life unimportant to her only months ago. But now she too was a woman, and knew what she really wanted and was going to have.
She was also a bit afraid; there was urgency; she may be with child. She had wanted to tell her sister, but Kit did not want to spoil the reunion with Honor and her husband Francis, she was so happy with his return and with the coming of their first child. Kit wanted to ask of the signs, how to be sure, she was pregnant, but she knew in her heart, she was. And where was John Paddon?

It was evening when she spotted the boats coming towards the island. She wanted to rush to meet them, but decided not to test her Fathers temper. She would wait till he returned to the house and had the hot meal Mother had prepared for him. Perhaps even wait until he had a mug of poteen in his hand. Yes, once he was relaxed and happy, she would ask him. Her Father sat down after dinner and lit his pipe; he then called to her to join him.
Your friend and my choice as your husband, has told me of some events that happened while I was away from the island...her heart beat quickly, had he found out about their meetings, did he know of her being with child?
She respected her Father so much, and always knew him to be smart and clever. Not much would get by him, and now she was in trouble.
I spoke with Liam Burke in town today. He has been looking for the fisherman Paddon. Seems Liam paid John Paddon to deliver a box to this island. Liam now believes the man did not keep his word as he believed the box should be in your possession. I have also told Liam he may call on you.

She was furious, yet could not show it. She knew the gift was delivered to the island, and she also knew she could not tell her father this. She would be caught in a lie. Could she change her story? Grandmother had allowed John Paddon to come to her house, and would tell Father. That may clear him of the suspicion of stealing, he could tell the truth and say the box is buried...That may clear his name, but would it allow for him to call on Kit? How was she to get this information to John? How could she get to see him?

The opportunity would present itself, as Honor was to go to the mainland hospital to have her baby, and a few of the women were allowed to accompany her.

Kit was sure to get herself on the boat to town, and somehow she would find John. She knew his home would be miles from the hospital, but she would plan that journey in time. First she must get off the island.

Kits Father went out early one morning and returned to the house with a guest, it was Liam Burke. He was dressed in his best clothes and that made Kit worry. He was so eager to speak with her. First he had to meet with Kit's Mother and was of course putting on his best manners. Finally he approached Kit.

I have come to apologize to you, Kit. Weeks ago I trusted a man to deliver something to you and he has gone off with it. It was a ring, one to promise you a future with me. Our fathers have approved of our marriage and we are going to begin our life together. I am going to get that ring back, believe me, and you will soon wear it on your finger.

She was shocked, angry and speechless. She did not want this boy. She did not!

So it was a ring in the box. She now felt determined to leave it buried, but she needed to clear the name of John Paddon.

She had only danced with Liam Burke at a few of the socials, never did she encourage him to have affection for her, her father had arranged this courtship, and she did not want anything to do with it. But she was not in the position to shame her family. She would be dishonoring her father by not accepting his choice.

What was to happen to her?

# The "Mullet"

- Belmullet
- Inishglora
- Inishkea North
- Co. Mayo
- Blacksod Bay
- Inishkea South
- Blackrock Lighthouse
- Tullagh Bay

That evening she spent getting Honor ready to make the trip to the hospital. She may not be due for a week or so, but because of the threat of ocean storms, she was to go while the sea was calm. Tomorrow was to be the day. Kit took the time that evening to speak with Honors husband, Francis Murphy, about the mainland. Seemingly just to pass the time, she asked about the tides and the Tullagh Bay, and asked if he had ever been there. He was able to inform her of the area; just enough to know that it would be a long journey, about six miles from the hospital by boat and it must be at high tide, as there was much bog in the area. She told him a good friend of hers lived in the area and she wanted to visit her once she got to the mainland; but asked him to please not tell her father, as he would probably not allow her go.

Her plan was coming together; she would be in town tomorrow for a few hours. She composed a letter to John that she would leave for him at the post office. She asked him to meet her the next time she came to town, or to come to the island as soon as he could. She had much to tell him, and wondered why he has stayed away.

Honor, Francis, Kit and another young man from the island, took off for the mainland in the morning. The sea was calm and they were soon at the harbor in Belmullet. The young man from the island took off for a good time in town while Kit, Honor and her husband hired a wagon to take them to the hospital. While they waited for Honor to be registered, Kit told them she so wanted to go to town for a bit, and it was agreed she would meet Francis later at the dock.

With letter in hand, she headed for the post. She kept her face covered with her shawl, as she did not want Liam Burke to know she was in town. A few familiar faces passed her on the street, yet she kept hidden. She had looked for John's boat at the harbor, but did not see it. She did look into every pub in town to perhaps find him; but no luck. Her only hope would be to get an answer from him after he got her letter.

On the trip back to the island, she told her brother-in-law, she would like to go to see her sister every time he goes, hoping to see John on one of the trips.

That night she wept, for the first time in a long time. She felt her life was not in her control anymore. Her Father, Liam Burke and mostly John Paddon had taken control, and she didn't like it.

A few trips were made to the island in the next week. There was no word from John and no sight of him. She had overheard her father speak of Liam searching for John Paddon, and the missing ring, but so far nothing more had been heard. Kit had a plan for the next time she was in town. She knew Honors husband would spend all the time there at the hospital and any other oarsman they brought with them would spend his time in the pub. She was going to take the boat and find Tullagh Bay. Everything was going as planned. After visiting Honor, Kit made some excuses and headed back to the dock. She was just as good handling a boat as a man, and the bay was calm today. She headed south and stayed as close to the shore as she could, as she did not want to miss the landmarks. She would see the Blackrock lighthouse on her right, and then she was to find the second inlet on her left and enter the small bay. She had to get by the sand bar and go further into the narrow streams between the bogs. The tide was high and it allowed her to easily search for any homes near the banks. She spotted a few buildings, two next to each other and one in the distance, alone. That would be his, as she knew him to be a solitary person. She cared not how much time had gone by, how she would get back or even what would happen if her father found out, she only thought of seeing John.
As she got closer to the shore she could see his boat, and she called to him. There was only silence but she proceeded. She tied the boat, got out and took a deep breath. She could soon be in his arms and her heart was pounding.

She knocked, and then opened the door. He was there, but on the floor, shaking and quivering! The fit! That is what they called his illness. She knelt beside him and wrapped her arms around him. Oh, he needed her and she so wanted him. She could care for him and perhaps could help stop this illness he has. She had no fear of him or this shaking. He soon became calm and she held him while he awoke. He looked terrible, his face was bruised and there was blood coming from his mouth. He was coming around and mumbled a bit, but nothing Kit could understand. At first he seemed not to recognize her, but as he slowly came to, he was quite surprised to see her there. He suddenly jumped to his feet and staggered backwards into a chair. She tried to approach him and he held her away. Why are you here, he asked?

She could barely understand his words, as he had bitten his tongue during the fit.
Why have you not come to see me? She asked. I have been waiting weeks to see you and was afraid you were hurt, now I can see you are. I want to help you.
Oh, girl you should not have come here. You should not see me this way. I was wrong to see you alone, and feel I have made a mistake. You should not be with me. We cannot be!
But I can help you, I can take care of you, I want to understand these fits, so we can get them fixed and stop this.

Kit, I am an epileptic, do you know what that is, and what it means? I cannot control these fits, they come at any time. A few weeks ago, I nearly drown, as I fell out of my boat during one. I was lucky to be near the shore and the tide was going out. My boat drifted out to sea and it took me hours to get home and days to retrieve my boat. I had bit my tongue, as I have today, yet it was a very severe bite, and that is why I speak poorly now. I could not face you in this condition. And you, my dear, cannot change or make better my epilepsy.
I do not care. I love you and came here to stay. I will never go home again. I am through with the island life. I want to belong to you.
They both sat in silence, not knowing what would come next. Kit had to ask.
Did you take the ring, the ring from Liam Burke?
The box? So that is what it held, a ring. It is on the island hidden near the well. You know I brought it there.
Liam says you stole it, and they are looking for you. My father also thinks you have it. And I asked his permission for you to call on me. How can he say yes if he thinks you are a thief? Please come to the island and clear this. Find the box and return it to Liam, before my father makes me accept the ring.

So your father wants you to have the young Burke, well that is probably for the best Kit.

But it cannot be, John as I am pregnant with your child.

He so very slowly sat up erect and turned his gaze at Kit. She had really surprised him with this. He shook his head and then dropped it into his hands. She knew he was crying, and she went to comfort him.

No, Kit, this is wrong and cannot be, I must think of what we can do.

We can marry, that is what we can do! If you have a wagon, we can ride tonight to Bangor and wed there. Or we can keep going, is what we can do. We can find ourselves a new life in the south, where we are not known. Please, John, take me away. I don't care about anything but you. You know how hard I can work and I am a good cook and I will be a good nurse to you as well. You can fish, and I will find work somewhere, please John, say you love me, say we can do this and we can start a new life.

There was no getting through to him; it was as if he could not hear her.

Come, we are going, going to the boats and then I'll get you back to the island. He walked out toward the water. Kit watched him walk away from her towards the boat and into the setting sun, the sky was beautiful, but she was filled with sadness, knowing this was to be an end.


Francis Murphy and Liam were also in a boat on the water. Liam had been following Kit through town without her seeing him. He saw her take the boat and ran to get Honors husband. Honor had given birth to a boy! Francis dismissed Liam, saying he was mistaken, that Kit would soon be at the hospital. But much time went by and it was Honor who urged her husband to go and look for Kit. She knew in her heart where she had gone but did not want to say so, with Liam present. It was getting dark, so, reluctantly Francis left; promising to return early tomorrow, with Honors parents to see their new grandson.
Francis joined Liam in his boat and they headed south, it was late in the day, and Francis did have concern for Kit out in a boat alone. Liam suggested they head towards the Blackrock lighthouse, as maybe she would go there.

Back in Tullagh Bay John and Kit were making their way through the bog, with her boat tied to his. Kit, not knowing what was to happen and not knowing what else to do, could only follow John's orders. He rowed them out past the sandbar and out into the bay. Was he taking her to her Father? Would he ask for her hand? Should she tell her father of herself being with child?

She sat quietly, rocking with the current, waiting for someone else to show the way.

As they approached the lighthouse, they saw another boat coming from the north. Someone lit a lantern and Kit heard her name being called. She knew it was Francis, but who was with him?
Oh no John, it is Liam Burke with my brother-in-law. Please do not stop, take me back to my Inishkea, I don't know what else to do.
All right, Kit, I'll do as you ask.
It must have been apparent to Francis and Liam that they were not going to stop, so they followed behind them and headed toward Inishkea. They could see a light at the harbor, so someone was there waiting. Kit was sure her father would be there as it was late and he surely was waiting for the news of Honor's child.
Francis called out to him, shouting he was a father, "the father of a son"!

All the boats seemed to arrive at the same time. John helped Kit out of the boat and proceeded to secure them. Francis and Liam pulled their boat up next to them. While Francis jumped out to embrace his father-in-law, Liam made a run for John and the first punch was thrown. Kits screaming did nothing to stop this encounter. It seemed John was letting this boy get the best of him, while her father Patrick and Francis watched.

Stop them Father, he is already hurt and not fighting back. He will give the ring to Liam, it is here on the island, he did not steal it, please father stop the fight!
Patrick let Liam get in some good punches, and then stepped in. Ok, men, lets get this matter straightened out tonight. John, is it true the box is here on the island? If so, we will find it now, right now.
The commotion brought out other people from their homes. Kit's Mother was walking toward them now. There was a time when Kit would have run to her, for comfort, but not now. She was suddenly aware of the separation she felt from all but John. Kit waited behind while the four men walked to the well.
What is the news of Honor, Kit?
Oh, Mum, she had a boy! A healthy boy!
And what of the men? What is going on?
Mum, I to marry John Paddon. And I shall not marry Liam Burke!

What are you saying girl, why do you want to marry that fisherman, you could have a good life with Liam, he has a home and a profitable business, he could give you anything you wanted. Besides, your father has decided.
No, he cannot and I will not! I will run away. I will!
Oh Kit, you cannot marry that man, he is a good man true, but not for you! He is the kind of man who prefers to live alone. And his illness is dangerous to be around.
The men returned. They talked of the agreement now to let the matter be settled. John Paddon was not guilty and was free to go. Liam had the ring, and was more than ready to give it to Kit, then and there. It was as if he needed John to see Kit accept it.
No, no Father, why has no one asked what I want? Cannot I decide whom I shall love and marry? I have the right to choose, I am a woman!
Ellen, bring your daughter home, and I shall end our dealings here with the men.
Off she went, her mother taking Kit's hand. What was to be decided, and settled? She knew this was not the end.
OK, then gentleman, off with the lot of you. I will settle this with my daughter and she will come to her senses. I shall not have so young a girl tell her father what to do. Give me a day or two and I will see you in town Liam, goodnight!

Patrick headed home and left Liam and John to depart from the island. John remained silent, yet Liam prodded and questioned, trying to find out what went on earlier that day. John rowed away leaving Liam perplexed. He would have to wait, wait for Mr. Ward to take care of the situation. Kit's mother tried to comfort her daughter, but as she saw it, it was just the whims of a girl, being suited by two men. Ellen thought mostly of her new grandson and how quickly she wanted to see him and her dear daughter Honor. Kit was left alone. The following day Ellen and Patrick set off for the mainland hospital to see the newborn. Kit declined the invitation to go, as she had decided to stay on the island for a few days, or at least until she had made a decision as to her future.
She took a long walk over the island, of which she seemed to have forgotten these last few months. Her "growing up" had taken her away from the freedom and beauty of this wonderful place. A place, for so many years, was her domain. Where she played and worked, invented games, people and events.

She would set out alone on her pony and in an hour could travel the perimeter of Inishkea pretending it was the whole world!

She had known such freedom and happiness. Why did she allow that to fade away? It was something of the past now, she would never feel that liberty again. Or of the control she had. That simple life was to be no more, a sad realization. She had chosen to be a woman. She gave herself to a man. A man she felt she loved, and believed he loved her. Was that a wrong decision? If so, it was too late to change things. What was she going to do? Why did John not fight for her? He had the opportunity to tell her father he loved her, why didn't he do so. He had shown her he wanted her so much, desired her so. He was gentle in making her a woman and she had trusted him.

She sat in the mist, waiting for answers. She heard the approaching voices on the water, and knew it must be her parents returning.

Their voices were full of laughter and joy. Daughter Honor had their first grandchild and they were so proud. It was a joyous time for the family. Kit was happy for her sister, yet she was consumed with her own worry. Her own life was in turmoil. When would be a good time to approach her father? Should she tell him now while he was happy? Perhaps then he would allow Kit to do what she wanted, choose her man. What would her mother think? Would she be just as happy with the knowledge of Kit's pregnancy?

Her parents were respected people on the island, and on the mainland. Many generations of Wards had lived here, and her Mothers family was well respected also.

She could see the boat arrive. There were four people in the boat; this meant Honor was home. They had discharged her from the hospital, and now the baby was here. Tonight was not to be the time to speak with father.

## BRIDGET GERRITY

Days were going by and no time seemed the right time to talk to father or mother. They were so happy with Honor and Francis and the baby Michael. Kit could not bring herself to disrupt their joy. She also did not want to burden Honor with her problems, so she was silent. Weeks were going by and she was silent. No sight of John Paddon, and her father seemed to have put the incident with Liam out of his mind.
But she had to do something, she was sure of her pregnancy now. She wanted to get to the mainland again, and try to get to John. She had no real friends on the mainland, but her Godmother did live there, and maybe she would help Kit. She was a nice woman, her mother's cousin, Bridget Gerrity. Kit asked her father if he would take her to visit, and asked if she would be allowed to stay for a while.
Perhaps he thought it was time for Kit to be off the island. Maybe she could rekindle the relationship with Liam. And maybe she needed to be around people her age.
He told Kit he would speak with Bridget and see if she would go along with the plan.
Within a few days it was arranged for Kit to go and stay with her Godmother, for a few days at least. Bridget's daughter Margaret and her husband had recently married and soon afterward left for America. The Gerrity home felt empty, so they were happy to have Kit's company.
Kit packed a few items and her Father took her to the mainland. They were both quiet on the ride over. Perhaps her father was feeling a bit of concern for his daughter, but it appeared he wanted to please Kit. She wanted so much to tell her Father, the state she was in. But she was afraid, afraid mostly of what he might do to John Paddon. So she kept her feelings and thoughts to herself. It was good to see Bridget; she was such a happy person, always smiling. She gave Kit a big hug and helped her into the house. She led Kit to her daughter's former bedroom and said to make herself at home. It would be good to have some female company again, and Kit was already wondering when and where she would tell Bridget of her story. She felt sure she would help.

Early one morning, Kit and Bridget were baking bread in the kitchen; they had mixed the dough and were sitting by the warm fire while the bread had time to rise.

This was the time Kit thought, No one would be home for hours, so it would give them plenty of time to talk it out.  Now where to begin?
Bridget, if I found myself in some trouble, would you send me home or try to help me? I feel I need to ask that before we go any further.
Bridget looked in wonder at Kit for a good bit of time.
So is this a problem that your father and mother are not aware of?  And one you feel I will be more tolerant of? I do love you like a daughter you know.  And have not been without some troubles in my own family.  No, I would not send you home Kit. You can share your problem with me.

I am pregnant, Bridget, and it is by a man whom my father does not approve of.  My father does not know I have been with him. He only thinks I have a teenage crush on him.  My father thinks I am still a girl, an innocent girl at that.  He wants me to marry Liam Burke and I do not love him.  I love John Paddon!

John Paddon!  Oh Kit, he is an old man!

Only forty-five Bridget!

And you are only sixteen Kit!

But he loves me I know it!  He came to see me many times and was good and gentile with me. I know he cares, but father has sent him away, there was a misunderstanding and father thought he was a thief, and Liam punched him in the face and was screaming and no one cared....

Kit, there is more to your fathers decision than that.  John Paddon has never been married, as no woman could trust him, never knowing what his illness would do to her. He becomes violent, and may hurt you.  He has been found many times in town, bloody and bruised and dirty from spending a night in a field.  Not knowing what has happened to him.... how could a woman trust to be near him?  You are a young girl, and should have a young man as a husband.

But I think you are right, your father will be very upset and ashamed. And your Mother will not take this well. But I will stand by you as I promised when I became your Godmother. We will find a way to tell your parents.

But, I cannot agree that you should wed John Paddon. Also my dear, I do not think you can hope for any forgiveness from Liam Burke. You have not made an easy future for yourself. Your parents may not take you back to the island, they are very proud and respected people, and this will be a great shock for them. It would be best if I tell them. I will plan a visit.

Kit fell to her knees at Bridget's feet, sobbing. Bridget patted her head, trying to console her. She offered words of encouragement; some day she will be forgiven and these difficult times will pass. She will also have a child to love and her life would be full of happiness.

But Bridget knew of the hardships to come and these words of comfort would be more difficult to speak in the months ahead.

The weeks to follow were quite lonely for Kit. Bridget met with Ellen and Patrick and told them of Kit's situation, and, as expected, they were heartbroken. Her father was so ashamed of the daughter he loved so much. She was such an adventurous and independent girl, he loved that about her, and now it was the reason he could not bring himself to see her again. Her Mother took the news a little easier, as she was never too surprised by her independent daughter's behavior. She did want to have Kit return home, but her husband would not allow it. It brought them great shame.

Kit spent the next months helping her godmother and her husband with their fishing business. Kit helped repair fishing nets, and did all she could around the house.

She spent the rest of her time walking to the beach and staring out to the island of Inishkea. She often cried to think she would never go back again. Her life would never be the same; she left her childhood behind, and was soon to become a mother.

There was no word from John Paddon, and upon learning of Kits pregnancy, Liam too withdrew his attention. The life her Father had planned for her and the life she dreamed of with a man she loved were never to happen. She brought shame to her family, and was now shunned by the only other man she really loved, her Father. She also was ashamed of herself, and she was so thankful to Bridget for taking her in.

She and Bridget decided the delivery of her child would take place at the workhouse in Belmullet. The workhouse was used by thousands during the famine, but now used for orphans and unwed mothers. It was managed by Nuns and paid for by the government. It was austere and the rules were strict. Everyone was awakened at 6a.m., out of their rooms at 6:30, breakfast at 8:30, lunch 2p.m., supper at 6p.m. And they were locked in the dormitories at 8p.m, lights out! All worked for room and board. The boys did all of the outside work, tending the chickens and goats, fixing the roof and any other jobs the Nuns could find for them. The girls worked in the laundry, as that was a business run out of the workhouse. The hospital, the Inn in town and the wealthy were their customers. The boys were given an education there, but the girls were deemed unworthy.

Clothing was provided, but boots were only given to the boys. If the girls were to be allowed to go to town, they carried their shoes until they arrived, wore them in town, and were expected to walk back barefoot. Some girls were lucky enough to leave shortly after they gave birth, but others lived for years in the workhouse. They lived under demanding conditions, working eight to twelve hours a day in the hospital, nursery, laundry or kitchen. They were separated from their children for all that time, only seeing the child at the end of the day. The children spent the majority of time with the Nuns.

## SEPTEMBER 1881

Kit's daughter Mary was born on September 6th. Kit went through the delivery without any family or friend to support her. She had gone to the workhouse one-week prior and word did not get to Bridget until after the baby was born. It was a painful, frightening experience but once the baby was placed in Kit's arms, she forgot it all.

What a beautiful child! Surely, Kit's Mother and Father would have to love this child. Once they saw her they would ask her to move back to Inishkea and live there forever. Then her daughter could live the free and happy life she had as a child. The sea, grassland and never-ending sky could all be hers. She would give her a pony, lambs, kittens, puppies anything she wanted! She would give it all to her precious daughter.

Kit spent the next two years living in the workhouse. The child had been cared for by the Nuns until Kit regained her strength and was able to work. She was able to see her daughter only after her chores were done. Scrubbing floors, washing loads of laundry and cooking took up much of her day. The child was to be baptized there in the workhouse, the Nuns giving Mary the middle name Magdalen; chosen by them because Kit was an unwed mother. Life in the workhouse was dismal and difficult. The only joy Kit felt was when she could be with her child. She so wished she could be on Inishkea, and show her young girl the beauty of the ocean and the island. She now understood her mistakes. Her life was changed and she had no idea of what her future would hold. No young suitors and no father for her child. But there was to be good news! The Gerrity's invited Kit back into their home, her Godmother had visited occasionally, and she saw the lonely existence Kit was living.

She had been back at Bridget's home for several weeks when they were to get an unexpected visit. Kit's parents had arrived. It was a tearful reunion. Kits Mother was the first to embrace her daughter, and they both cried. Her father stood silently and Kit approached him slowly.

I am so sorry Father, she said sobbing. He put his arms out to her and they too hugged and cried. She had not seen them for such a long time and she loved them so. Had they forgiven her? Was she to return home?

But the three adults had already made plans for Kit and Mary Magdalen. They were to travel to America when arrangements were made. Bridget's daughter and her husband had invited her to join them in their Pennsylvania home. Kit was to start a new life. Away from the stares and criticism of her peers, away from the men who no longer wanted to be a part of her life, away from her mistakes.

To aide the Irish who wanted, or needed to travel to America, a relief fund had been set up by the Quakers and a minister, James Tuke. A substantial part of the cost had to be provided by the traveler, and Kit's family had been saving for quite some time.

A ship to Canada was less expensive than to America, so Kit and Mary Magdalen were to go to Montreal where there were relatives of the Gerritys. From there she would travel south to the United States to live with Bridget's daughter. Many preparations had yet to be made and some time would be needed before she would leave, giving Kit once again time to be with her Mother and Father, and to once again be on her beautiful Inishkea.

### THREE YEARS LATER

Honor and Bridget waved from the dock at Kit who stood out on the deck of the great steamship Devonia. The ship from the Allan Line was on its way from Sligo to Montreal, Canada. She was to be met by cousins of the Gerrity's who would help her to go on to the United States where Kit was to start her new life. Little Mary was held in her arms, and she too would have a new life, she too was leaving her past behind. It was an exciting adventure for them both, and that anticipation made the farewells a bit easier. Of course all were crying and it was especially hard on Bridget, who was loosing to America two more of her girls! Honor herself had her own desires to leave for America.

The trip would take at least one week, and passengers were to provide their own provisions except for water. So, baskets of bread, cheese, smoked fish and apples were of more importance than trunks of clothes, which for Kit was not an issue, as she wore her best clothes and had not much more. Some young boys had helped her carry the necessities to the women's cabin, as she was afraid to let go of Mary's hand. They were to share the bunk, in a ward of just women. Most were just as frightened as Kit, so they seemed to look out for each other. Many spoke

Irish, but there were other women with interesting dress and strange languages in the group.  Beds were placed inches away from the next one, not leaving much room to walk.  At the end of the room were toilets and some showers.  Luggage and food was kept under your bunk in locked drawers.  The ship was noisy, with the diesel engines running, and it smelled, from the fuel and the exotic food!  Kit made the acquaintance of the ladies in the bunks next to hers.  They too had small children, but their husbands were in the compartments with all the men.  Kit decided to take one last walk on the deck, as she felt she would be much safer below after they got underway.  The ship had already been making its way out of the bay and the setting sun lie before her. What was out there for her, what promise?  A fresh start, they all said, you can begin a new life. But what was before her was vast and frightening.  She quickly turned back to see her homeland.  Tears filled her eyes as she watched the green of Ireland fade into the darkness.  Brokenhearted, she lifted her sweet daughter and hugged her to her breast.  Mary pointed her finger in the direction of the sunset,    Mommy, look how pretty America is!

# The Ballina Journal,
## And Connaught Advertiser.

THE BALLINA JOURNAL, MONDAY, FEBRUARY 25, 1886

[Registered] | PRICE ONE PENNY

## ALLAN LINE

**Royal Mail Steamers to UNITED STATES & CANADA FROM LONDONDERRY.**

SARDINIAN... For Quebec & Montreal...Sept 14
PARISIAN...... For Quebec & Montreal...Sept 21
CIRCASSIAN... For Quebec & Montreal...Sept 29
POLYNESIAN...For Quebec & Montreal...Oct 5
SARMATIAN.. For Quebec & Montreal...Oct 13

Rates of Ocean Passage:
Cabin 10 to 18 Guineas | Intermediate, £6 6s.
Steerage at Lowest Rates.

Through Tickets special rates to Chicago, Winnipeg (Manitoba), North-West Territory, and to all points in the Western States and Canada.

To TOURISTS SPORTSMEN, and others— Round Trip Tickets combining Excursionists to Niagara Falls and other places of interest in the United States and Canada, the wonderful scenery in the Rocky Mountains and the Sporting districts of British Columbia.

## "ANCHOR" LINE.

**AMERICAN MAIL STEAMSHIPS.**

Cheapest, Fastest, and best-routes
To New York, Philadelphia, Boston,
BALTIMORE & HALIFAX.
Lowest Through Rates
TO MANITOBA AND CANADA
And all Points in the United States.
Glasgow to New York every Thursday.
LONDONDERRY to NEW YORK DIRECT
Every Friday, as under :

| | | | | |
|---|---|---|---|---|
| s s Devonia | ...4270 | Tons | Friday, | Feb 26 |
| s s Circassia | ...4271 | Tons | Friday, | Feb 16 |
| s s Ethiopia | ...4004 | Tons | Friday, | Feb 22 |
| s s Anchoria | ...4167 | Tons | Friday, | March 1 |
| s s Furnessia | ...5496 | Tons | Friday, | Mar. 8 |
| s s Devonia | ...5496 | Tons | Friday, | Mar. 15 |
| s s Circassia | ...4167 | Tons | Friday, | Mar 22 |
| s s Ethiopia | ...4004 | Tons | Friday, | Mar. 29 |

And Weekly Thereafter

Passengers are in good time to embark

The above Steamships are despatched from New York to Londonderry Direct every Saturday.

FARES—Saloon Specially Reduced
£9 9s £10 10s and £12 12s.
To NEW YORK, BOSTON, PHILADELPHIA.—Second Class (Second Class Cabin), including all necessaries, and Third Class (Steerage) at Lowest Rates.

Passengers booked at Lowest Rates to all

## THE JOURNEY

On ship, the women in the beds around her wanted to know all about each other. Did they know people in America, did they have jobs, and did they have the proper papers?

Some women had no papers of identity at all. They had paid off someone on ship to get him or her on board. There were mothers, sisters, daughters, teachers, weavers, nurses and prostitutes. All willing to share their stories, some needed to make friends, as most were scared to death of making this trip. There were many horror stories about crossing the Atlantic, and many were afraid of dying at sea, during the famine when over one million Irish emigrated, they were called the coffin ships. So the women talked, and got to know each other. They were sure to want to know the story of the young Kit and her daughter. She told them of the death of her young husband, who drown in the sea, he was a fisherman. She was going to America to live with his relatives, who were quite well off and could provide for Kit and her child. She had the sympathy of everyone; as a young widow, and with such a young child, what a shame.

And what is your name dear?

I, I am Katherine Paddon and this is my daughter Mary Magdalen.

Kit and Mary made the journey across the Atlantic. It was a wonderful sight to see land, and at the harbor she was met by her Godmothers relatives. They were an older couple, without children of their own. They had a large house and owned a factory in town. They had assisted many people coming from Ireland, as they knew the conditions there. Life had not gotten much easier in Ireland since they themselves left not long after the famine.
Many of the people they helped had gone south to the coal regions of Pennsylvania in the United States. There were jobs in the mines and there were also silk mills. These were the mills where many women worked.

After a few days, the couple asked Kit to join them in the garden for a talk. Little Mary Magdalen played while they approached her with an offer. They would help Kit by giving her money to start her new life in America if she would give them her daughter! Kit was shocked, how could they expect her to give away her child?
It would be best for little Mary, they stressed, and no one in Kit's future would have to know of the illegitimate child. She could go to America and marry and have more children. They have helped her begin a new life and she should feel obligated to them! They could give Mary a good life, as they already had the means.
No! No was the answer, she could not give away her daughter, Whether Kit had a husband or not, Mary was hers! Someone from Pennsylvania had better come soon, or she would walk there herself.

Some days later, after traveling by train, she arrived in Port Griffith, Pennsylvania. She was greeted by Bridget's daughter Margaret.
Come Kit and I will introduce you to everyone. Kit quickly whispered in her ear, if you would please, I am to be known as Kit Paddon. If I am to start a new life, I want my daughter to have a proper name. Please!

Of course Kit, everything is possible here in America!
It was a small house near the top of a hill, overlooking the town. Kit was given her own room, with a small bed and a cot for Mary. It was great to hear the Irish language again.

There were mostly women living in the house, from very old to Mary being the youngest. Three of the girls were Kit's age, and they became fast friends. Kit was to find some work in the silk mills, as she had a few years of experience in weaving and knitting. Because the house was full of women, there was always someone who could watch the young children.

Mary Magdalen would be able to go to the school in town. Something Kit was never able to do. Port Griffith was a small but prosperous town. The Susquehanna River ran through it, and two grand bridges could take you to the western lowlands. On that side of the bridge were farms with dairy cattle, but not a sheep to be found! The mountains were large and covered with trees; Kit had never seen so many trees. The towns also were different, as they were made of red bricks! And they were several stories tall. The two-story workhouse was the tallest structure in Bellmullet.

On the weekends, the Irish of the community on the hill, above the railroad junction, gathered together. It was a time to speak Irish, talk, sing the songs and tell the tales of the homeland. There were quite a few immigrants, mostly young people, who were working to earn enough money to bring their families to America.

It was during one of these weekend gatherings that Kit met Peter McAndrew. He was a war hero who lived as a border in a neighbor's house. He already knew her as the young widow with the pretty daughter, and was quick to introduce himself. Their relationship began then and there. And the courtship did not last long before Peter asked her to marry him. It was a wonderfully happy time for Kit. Her new life had begun.

Two years had passed since Kit left Ireland. Letters arrived from Bridget, Honor and even Kit's Mother telling of their life back in Inishkea.

There had been a terrible storm on the Atlantic and many areas of the island were completely destroyed. Twenty people were killed, by the waves or by being crushed in their homes. The government decided to move all the inhabitants off the island to the mainland. The Wards and all of the other families on the island had to move.

They were given some money for their properties and many had to decide what would be best for them now. Some had relatives on the mainland and stayed there. Some took the money and immigrated; America, England and Australia were the destinations of choice.

Kit wept with joy when told her Father, Mother, Honor and her family had decided to come to America. They had never regained their respect form the mainland community after what happened to Kit.

Her Father had other reasons to leave as well. And he wanted to leave quickly. He had become a very bitter man in the last few years. His daughter was scorned by the community and ultimately had to leave her homeland. John Paddon, the father of her child, did not care about Kit or Mary. Word was he had taken work on a fishing vessel and had not been seen in quite some time. But Patrick heard that Paddon had returned home. He had a plan for John Paddon, and it was to take place soon, as the Ward family was soon to leave for America.

## TULLAGH BAY

Anthony, Patrick's son was nineteen now and a tall, strong man he had become. Anthony had also harbored a hatred for the man who caused his sister to leave Ireland.

There was a debt to be paid by John Paddon as he had broken apart the Ward family. Patrick and Anthony took their currach out for a trip to Tullagh Bay, where they would find Paddon. It was near dark when they spotted his boat coming in towards the sand bar. They had dropped their anchor as close to his home as they could and Patrick laid low in the boat. John would recognize Patrick, but he never knew Anthony, so he would be the one to speak. When Paddon was close enough, Anthony called out to him.

Hello there! Do you think you could help me, I just need a good pull and I'll be off the sand bar here.

John told the young man he was a fool to be in the waters if he hadn't know how to get himself about, but he turned his boat and headed towards an unknown fate.

Patrick was holding the oar, and just the sound of Paddon's voice made him tighten his grip. Anthony whispered, not yet Father, hold on, he shall be here soon.

Soon you shall have your revenge, soon he will pay for the loss of your daughter and grandchild, and he shall pay for taking them away form Ireland.

Soon you shall end your shame, and end the life of John Paddon!

# The Ballina Journal, And Connaught Advertiser.

THE BALLINA JOURNAL, MONDAY SEPTEMBER 17 1888

**BALLINA, MONDAY 17, 1888.**

On Tuesday last Robert Mostyn, Esq., Coroner, held an inquest at Bangor on the body of John Padden. The circumstances surrounding the death were mysterious. He absented himself from his home on the 2nd, and his body was found in an upright position in about 10 feet of water on the 9th. The large discoloured mark on the shoulder showed that he must have come into contact with something previous to death. It transpired from the evidence that he had been subject to epileptic fits, and the doctor having certified that the death resulted from suffocation. A verdict accordingly.

Patrick Ward had decided to take his family to Sligo by boat; this would allow them to avoid the mainland completely. With most of their belongings destroyed by the great storm, they had little to carry to America with them. The best of their clothes they wore and the rest were provisions for the trip over the Atlantic.

Many of the families from the north island were traveling to England, as they had family there, and the trip was less costly. But the Wards were drawn to America. Ellen must say goodbye to her numerous cousins, Aunts and Uncles. It was a terribly sad end to a wonderful life on Inishkea Island. But the rough, wild land and sea were to be returned to the seals, the birds, to nature. Man was not wanted.

Looking back as they rowed away, there was a tear in every eye. Their independent life was to be no more. Gone were the days of rich soil for the gardens, the abundant life of seafood, of lobster and crab, and the freedom from other men. They had once a life of plenty, and that life was gone.

Within days, the Ward family was on a ship heading to America, where they too would begin again.

Ireland lost many of its people because of the difficult times. The potato famine, which led to one million people leaving Ireland, and another one million who died of starvation and fever, changed Ireland forever. Whether to escape starvation, poverty, prejudice or a secretive past, all were brave enough to begin a new life in America. For one young woman and her child, it was a journey to freedom, where you could start a new life and create your own past. You were who you said you were and not many questions were asked.

Those that were forced to leave never lost the love for their country. It remained in their hearts and left a longing that was to be passed to the next generations. One hundred years later, driven by curiosity, family history and a fascinating vision of a young woman crossing the Atlantic Ocean with a child in her arms, I found the truth of my Grandmother and Great-Grandmother. I am proud to have come from such strong, independent and courageous women. My Father was not to know the true story of his Mother's life, but I think he too would be proud of her. Being an unwed mother was something to be ashamed of back in those days, and is still not well accepted. But I do believe Kit had her child out of the love she, as a very young woman, felt she had committed to, and wanted from the father of her child.

Her family never forgave John Paddon and could not perhaps forgive themselves for turning away from her, when she needed them most. They too came to America with secrets. They too started new lives, with new names, different dates, and small lies.

That was something they carried silently in themselves, as Mary Magdalen grew up to be a happy, healthy dignified young woman.

A true example of what America offered to someone, a beginning.

Deiriadh agus Tus

MARY MAGDALEN     1900

Katherine, Mary Magdalen, Joseph, Michael, Mary, Thomas Sr. & Thomas Jr.

## REFERENCES:

### UNITED STATES

National Archives, Washington, D.C.
Pennsylvania Division of Vital Records
Commonwealth of Pennsylvania Luzerne
    County : Marriage & Naturalization Records

### IRELAND

Ireland National Library, Dublin
Griffith's Primary Valuation of Tenements
National Church Tithe/Tax Books
Mayo/Sligo Records of Births, Baptisms &
    Death Registrations
Mayo North Family History Centre
Castlebar Library, County Mayo
Kilmore Erris Parish Baptismal Records
Belmullet Library/ Maps
  The Ballina Journal & Connaught Advertiser
    Actual newspaper articles:
      *The Steamship DEVONIA departure
        February, 1886
      *Coroner report: September 1888
Bangor Civil Register of Deaths 1997
  *John Paddon, a bachelor from Tullagh Bay, died on the 2$^{nd}$ of September 1888 at the age of 52. The cause of death was accidental drowning and was registered by theCoroner, Robert Moystyn. There was an inquest held in relation to this deathon the11$^{th}$ of September, 1888.